THE ADVENTURES OF

MERLIN

POTIONS AND
POISON

Also available:

The Magic Begins

Coming soon:

A Fighting Chance

Sword and Sorcery

For older readers:

The Dragon's Call

Valiant

Coming soon for older readers:

The Mark of Nimueh

The Poisoned Chalice

POTIONS AND POISON

Text by

Jacqueline Rayner

Based on the stories by

Julian Jones and Ben Vanstone

BANTAM BOOKS

MERLIN: POTIONS AND POISON
A BANTAM BOOK 978 0 553 82112 3

First published in Great Britain by Bantam,
an imprint of Random House Children's Books
A Random House Group Company

This edition published 2009

1 3 5 7 9 10 8 6 4 2

The Random House Group Limited supports the Forest Stewardship Council
(FSC), the leading international forest certification organization. All our titles that
are printed on Greenpeace-approved FSC-certified paper carry the FSC logo. Our
paper procurement policy can be found at www.rbooks.co.uk/environment.

Typeset in 16/22 Bembo Schlbk by Falcon Oast Graphic Art Ltd.

Bantam Books are published by Random House Children's Books,
61–63 Uxbridge Road, London W5 5SA

www.**kids**at**randomhouse**.co.uk
www.**rbooks**.co.uk

Addresses for companies within The Random House Group Limited can be found
at: www.randomhouse.co.uk/offices.htm

THE RANDOM HOUSE GROUP Limited Reg. No. 954009

A CIP catalogue record for this book is available from the British Library.

Printed in the UK by CPI Bookmarque, Croydon, CR0 4TD

With grateful thanks to
Johnny Capps, Julian Murphy,
Polly Buckle, Rachel Knight, Sarah Dollard,
Jamie Munro, Pindy O'Brien, Filiz Tosun,
Anna Nettle and Rebecca Morris

CONTENTS

CHAPTER ONE
THE EGG

The ancient cave was dark and eerie, the stuff of nightmares. The woman who now stood within it, however, was young and beautiful – or at least, that was how she appeared. Her name was Nimueh and she was a sorceress, and it was magic that gave her both youth and beauty.

Magic was forbidden in King Uther's realms, on pain of death. Like many sorcerers, Nimueh hated the king, but unlike most of them she did not fear him.

Instead, she planned that one day he would fear *her*. And that day might just be today . . .

Nimueh picked up a handful of clay and began to mould it into the shape of a small, hunched creature. When it was finished to her satisfaction, she carefully placed the model in a carved ivory and gold eggshell, muttering incantations all the while.

She stroked the egg, and her

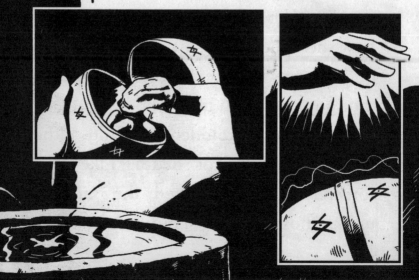

voice rose as the spell grew in power. This was magic of a kind few could master.

Beneath her fingers, the ivory became a sealed eggshell. It was still decorated with Nimueh's mark: four intersecting lines enclosing a single dot. From within the shell came a glow, outlining the silhouette of the clay model. And then there was something else – a light from the centre of the sculpture itself.

A glowing, beating heart.

The creature was alive.

In the middle of the cave was a carved column topped with a water-filled stone

basin. This was Nimueh's scrying bowl, through which she could observe the whole kingdom. Now she cast a further spell, creating a physical link with the world outside her cave, a passage between the bowl and the underground rivers that ran nearby. She tossed the egg into the basin and watched as the waters swirled it away. Her magic would make sure it went in the right direction. With a wave of her hand, the surface smoothed again, forming a picture of the egg's progress as it washed through underground rivers and streams until at last it surfaced in a pool – a pool beneath the citadel of Camelot.

Nimueh watched with glee as a tiny talon burst through the eggshell.

Oh yes, Uther would fear her now . . .

Somewhere far above the pool, inside Camelot itself, was the only sorcerer in the land more powerful than Nimueh. Unlike Nimueh, this magician really was as young as he looked. He worked for Prince Arthur, who had no idea of his servant's magical abilities, and also acted as general dogsbody to the elderly court physician, Gaius – who was only too aware that his charge was a magic-user, a warlock. The young lad's name was Merlin, and he was destined for great things.

However, despite his great powers, Merlin had no idea that a strange egg had hatched below only hours before. Right now, he was looking at a dead body lying face down on the street.

'Aren't you scared?' he asked Gaius, who was kneeling beside the corpse.

'Of what?' Gaius replied.

'That you might catch whatever it is.'

The doctor shook his head. 'This is part of my job. Anyway, most of the time there's

really nothing to be scared of.' He reached out a hand and rolled over the body – revealing unnaturally pale skin webbed with blue veins, and milky white eyeballs. They both stared in horror.

'You were saying . . . ?' Merlin commented as Gaius hurriedly threw a blanket over the corpse before anyone else noticed its bizarre appearance. They loaded the body onto a cart and made their way

towards the castle, whereGaius had his chambers. Both men avoided looking at passers-by, trying desperately not to draw attention to themselves – if word of this got out, there would be panic in Camelot.

'What are you doing?' called a girl's voice.

Merlin tried unsuccessfully to hide the cart behind him as a young woman came up to them. It was Gwen, maid to the king's ward, Morgana. She was carrying a small posy, and as usual she was smiling.

'Just moving something,' Merlin replied. He quickly changed the subject. 'Someone given you flowers?'

'Oh – no. They're for Lady Morgana.' She plucked a bloom out of the bunch. 'Would you like one? Here – a purple one. Purple suits you. Not that I'm saying red doesn't suit you,' she added hurriedly, as Merlin tucked the flower into his red tunic. He felt a little silly, but it seemed to make Gwen happy. She waved cheerfully as he set off again, pushing his dead burden.

'Do you think it could be some kind of plague?' Merlin asked later as Gaius examined the body in the privacy of his chambers.

The doctor shook his head. 'No, I fear something like this could never come from nature. But who has this kind of power?'

'You think it's caused by *magic*?'

Gaius was about to reply when a call of 'Merlin!' cut him off. Merlin went to see who it was. Prince Arthur was standing in the doorway. Had he heard them talking about magic? Merlin wondered. It seemed not. 'Tell Gaius that my father wants to see him now,' Arthur said. Then he raised his eyebrows, staring quizzically at the flower in Merlin's tunic.

'Oh . . .' said Merlin, hurriedly discarding the bloom. 'Er, Gwen gave it to me.'

The prince was shaking his head as he left the room.

'Why couldn't Arthur have just given you the message himself?' Merlin asked as Gaius – who had clearly heard every word – got up to leave.

'Because that's the way it is,' said the doctor. 'You're a servant.'

Merlin was irritated. He might be a servant, but he'd been told he was destined to help Arthur become the greatest king the world had ever known! He'd already used his magic to save the prince's life at least twice, and he'd thought they were becoming – well, not friends exactly, but maybe . . . allies? He thought they had begun to understand each other, at least. But it seemed Arthur could switch that on and off at will, sometimes friendly, sometimes every inch the haughty prince, and Merlin felt quite annoyed about it. 'If he knew who I was, what I've done for him . . .' he grumbled.

'. . . you'd be a dead servant,' Gaius reminded him.

Merlin sighed. Recognition – or staying alive. It was a tough choice.

CHAPTER TWO
PLAGUE IN CAMELOT

A servant was lying on the floor of the council chambers. His skin was pale and patterned with blue veins, and his eyes were milk-white orbs. He had been dead only a few minutes and the surrounding courtiers were silent with shock.

After examining him, Gaius stood up and turned to King Uther. 'Sire, this is the second case today. I've seen nothing like it before.'

'What's the cause?' the king asked.

Gaius hesitated, knowing that the king

would be furious at the answer he was about to give. But he had no choice; not if people were dying. 'I think you'd have to say that the most likely cause is sorcery.'

Uther froze, but only for a moment. Then he turned to Prince Arthur. 'You must find who did this. Conduct door-to-door searches and double the guards on all the gates. And lend the physician your servant.'

Arthur didn't look happy. 'Merlin! But—'

'Gaius has to find a cure. He needs all the help we can give him.' The king was icily calm, but no one could doubt the fury beneath. 'If Gaius is right, this city will be wiped out. This is the kind of magic that undermines our authority, challenges all we've done. If we cannot control this plague, people will turn to magic for a cure. We have to find this sorcerer – and quickly.'

In a matter of hours Camelot had

changed from a happy, bustling city to a place of fear and death.

Merlin and Gaius had seen people at death's door and the old physician felt helpless. The number of corpses in the streets continued to increase. It was the city guard who had to carry them away, in between their searches of every room of every house in every street. Doors were kicked down if no one was at home − or if the occupants just took too long to answer the guards' knocks.

Passers-by were grabbed and made to empty their pockets and bags.

In Gaius' chambers, Merlin was watching as the doctor examined a victim's stomach contents, in the hope that they might discover how the disease was being spread.

'What I don't understand,' the boy said, 'is why someone would use magic like this.'

Gaius sighed. 'Magic corrupts,' he said. 'People use it for their own ends.'

But Merlin hadn't been corrupted by magic – he knew he hadn't. 'Not all magic is bad,' he insisted.

'It's neither good nor bad itself. It's how you use it.'

Merlin thought about that. In the same way that a knife could be used to cut bread and cheese or stab a man, and water could either quench a man's thirst or drown him, a spell could either harm or heal. He knew dark magic existed – spells that could do terrible things. But the darkness was in the person who chose to use them, who decided that because they had the power, they also had the right to do evil. In the hands of such people, perhaps even the most benevolent of enchantments could be used for wicked purposes. So wicked people did wicked things with magic, and good people did good things – or did they? If Gaius was right, magic made you do bad things just because you could.

Merlin was about to question Gaius further when the chamber door was smashed open.

The two men looked up, startled, as guards entered and began to throw equipment and books to the floor. Gaius opened his mouth to protest – and then noticed that Prince Arthur had come into the room behind the guards. This was an official visit and it would not be wise to object.

'I'm sorry, Gaius. We're searching every room in the town for the sorcerer,' the prince said.

'And why would he be here?' Gaius asked.

Arthur looked slightly embarrassed. 'I'm just doing my job. We have to look for any evidence suggesting the use of enchantments. What's this room up here?'

He was standing at the bottom of the stairs leading to Merlin's room.

'It's mine,' Merlin said, suddenly terrified. He knew where 'evidence suggesting the use of enchantments' could be found, and it was right by his bed. Gaius had given Merlin a book of spells, and he'd been reading it the night before. He could see that Gaius had realized this too, and they exchanged a look of horror as

Arthur climbed the stairs. It was obvious that the prince didn't really expect to find anything in Merlin's room, and was a little fed up about having to search everywhere. But he took his duties seriously. Recently, two separate attempts had been made on Arthur's life using magic, and he wouldn't be feeling too kindly towards sorcerers. Merlin's only hope was that the book was hidden under some of the mess littering his room, and that Arthur didn't search too carefully.

'Merlin, come here!' Arthur called a moment later.

Merlin almost stopped breathing in shock. This was the end. But he knew he had to respond to his master's command. If he tried to run, the guards would cut him down. He hurried up the stairs, his heart beating so fast he thought it might burst out of his chest.

WHAT'S THIS ROOM?

IT'S MINE

LOOK WHAT I'VE FOUND!

'Look what I've found,' Arthur announced, and Merlin waited for the guards to be summoned, the arrest, the execution ... 'I've found a place where you can put things,' the prince continued. 'It's called a cupboard.'

IT'S CALLED A CUPBOARD, WHERE YOU CAN PUT THINGS AWAY!

Merlin relaxed, giving Arthur a sheepish smile. But thank goodness for the mess: it had hidden the book! He glanced down at the floor — and his heart nearly exploded again. *The book could still be seen.* It was

lying by the bed, quite, quite visible, just by Arthur's feet. All Arthur had to do was look down – and an execution, Merlin's execution, would be taking place.

CHAPTER THREE
DOING GOOD

Prince Arthur was still glancing around Merlin's room, tutting at the state of it. Any second now, he would see the magic book.

Merlin took his life in his hands. With Arthur standing next to him, searching for evidence of sorcery – Merlin *cast a spell*.

He whispered so quietly it couldn't be heard, his lips barely moving. A tunic slid from the bed, falling neatly over the book. When Arthur bent down a few seconds later, the book was covered – and the prince, obviously not feeling it was necessary to examine every item in his servant's room, didn't notice it.

With a final 'tut' at the mess, Arthur left the room and returned to Gaius' chambers.

'How long d'you think it may be before you find a cure?' Merlin heard him ask.

'Depends on how many interruptions I get,' came the doctor's pointed reply.

'Of course. I'm sorry.'

Merlin came down the stairs just in time to see Arthur beckon to the guards. 'Come on, we're finished here.'

Gaius turned to Merlin the second the door was shut. 'We have to hide that book.'

'No.' Merlin was quite certain. 'We must *use* it.'

'You want to practise magic when the king is hunting for sorcerers? Are you mad?'

But to Merlin it seemed simple. 'I could cure that man we saw.'

Gaius sighed. 'I know it's tempting to use the way you find easiest, Merlin, but it's no good just curing one person – we have to discover how this illness is spreading.'

'Arthur's out there right now looking for the sorcerer,' Merlin reminded him, but Gaius shook his head.

'A sorcerer powerful enough to do this will never be found by searching the town,' he said. 'We just have to hope that science can find the answer – before this kills us all.'

In her lair, Nimueh stared into the scrying bowl. She could see the rows upon rows of dead bodies that had been collected in Camelot's main square, and they made her smile. Uther would be scared now, so scared. She had watched as he ordered Prince

Arthur to isolate the lower town, where most of the victims were from. This wouldn't work, she knew, because the disease didn't really come from there. However, if the lower town really had contained the source of the illness, the king would have simply condemned to death everyone who lived there. Such ruthless behaviour didn't surprise Nimueh, though. She knew Uther's ways.

As it was, she knew that even this wouldn't save him; wouldn't save the people of Camelot from the horrific deaths she had planned for them. She bore them no malice – but as Uther's subjects, loyal to the king, their fate was decided. Uther had to suffer – as she had suffered.

Then the picture on the water changed, and her startling blue eyes shone with pleasure as she gazed down at her creation, the creature of clay – the true cause of the

disease. It was no longer a tiny hunched baby. It had grown into a monster. Even if it were discovered, it could never be destroyed. Her plan was foolproof.

'What's different about this victim?' Gaius asked. It sounded like he'd made a discovery, and Merlin hurried over to see what he was looking at.

The dead body on Gaius' workbench was dressed in a velvet robe, a jewelled pendant hanging round her neck.

'She's a woman,' Merlin pointed out.

Gaius raised his eyes to the ceiling.

'Sometimes I wonder if your magical talents were given to the right person.' He gestured to the body. 'Anything else?'

'Er . . .' Merlin took in the clothes and jewellery. 'She's a courtier. But how does that help us?'

'Most of the cases are from the lower town – but courtiers rarely go there. She probably hasn't met anyone else who has the disease, which suggests the disease isn't spread by contact.'

Merlin nodded, realizing what Gaius was getting at. 'And courtiers would eat different food from the townspeople too.'

'So what's the only thing they do share?' the doctor asked – and then Merlin noticed a bucket standing by the bench.

'Water.' Of course! The townspeople and the nobles all got their water from the same source. But the townspeople drank the most – the nobles could afford wine and

ale — which was why more of them had
fallen ill. 'You think the disease is spread
through water!' he cried.

'Merlin, you're a prodigy,' Gaius said with
a smile.

Merlin headed off to the pump to collect a
water sample. He felt quite cheerful. Now
they'd worked it out — well, all right, now
Gaius had worked it out — it would only be
a matter of time before they stopped the
disease in its tracks.

He was close to Gwen's house, and reflected
on how much had happened since they'd
bumped into each other only the day
before. The girl did act strangely at times
— like giving him flowers and getting all
embarrassed — but she was so kind and
gentle that you couldn't help liking her.

As he was pumping the water, the door
to Gwen's house opened. Merlin looked

up, expecting to see either Gwen or her father, Tom the blacksmith, setting off for work. But instead, Gwen ran out into the street, a look of horror on her face, her eyes streaming with tears. She dashed past Merlin, not even noticing him. Picking up his pail of water, Merlin hurried after her.

He followed Gwen to Gaius' chambers. For a moment he felt utter dismay – if Gwen needed a doctor, perhaps she had the sickness! But it wasn't Gwen who was ill.

'My father! Please, Gaius, he's all I have!' she was begging.

PLEASE, GAIUS, HE'S ALL I HAVE!

Merlin felt terrible as Gaius told the weeping girl that he couldn't help. A few minutes ago everything had seemed so simple – all they had to do was find a cure. Ha! Suddenly that seemed like the most impossible task in the world. And even if they succeeded – it would be too late to save Gwen's father.

He couldn't bear feeling so helpless; he just couldn't stand it!

When Merlin had first used sorcery to save Prince Arthur's life, Gaius had told him that must be the purpose of his magic. That had seemed to make sense at the time – after all, Arthur was supposed to become a great king one day. But surely there was more to Merlin's magic than that. It couldn't be right to save only Arthur's life, and let other people – good people – die, just because they weren't royal or weren't destined to do important things.

Magic could be either good or bad, depending on who used it and why. But surely choosing *not* to use magic could be either good or bad too. In this case it had to be bad. Because if he didn't use it, Tom would die, and Gwen would never smile again.

CHAPTER FOUR
A MAGICAL CURE

Merlin had hidden the magic book under a floorboard after Arthur's search, and Gaius had told him not to get it out again until the hunt for the sorcerer was over. But that was clearly ridiculous. How could Merlin possibly let his friend suffer so badly when he might be able to help her? If magic had made Gwen's father ill, then magic would cure him.

Merlin waited until he heard Gaius snoring, then pulled the book from its hiding place and began to read.

It took the young warlock only a few minutes to find exactly what he needed. It took him just over an hour to collect the materials he required and cast the enchantments, creating a small cloth-wrapped poultice that twinkled as though it contained a thousand dancing fireflies. It took another half-hour to reach Gwen's house, avoiding the patrolling guards on the way. Then he magically opened her front door and slipped the enchanted poultice under her father's pillow. He left the Smithy, but waited for a while, watching through the window to see the look of amazement and joy on Gwen's face as she woke to find her father well again. And then he made his way back to the palace.

The disease had been killing people for two days. But in less than two hours,

Tom the blacksmith had been cured.

Merlin overslept the next morning, and was glad that Gaius wasn't around when he finally made it downstairs – he didn't want to explain why he was smiling so much. A note told him that the doctor had gone to tell King Uther the results of his experiments with the city's water.

Merlin hurried to the Lady Morgana's chambers, hoping to find Gwen there. He was in luck. There she was, smiling and humming as usual as she tidied up the room. She turned and beamed at Merlin as he put his head round the door.

'How's your father? Is he feeling better?' the boy asked, knowing the answer already.

'Yes! It's incredible. It's a miracle!' she cried.

'Great,' Merlin said, grinning.

Gwen's smile didn't fade, but she appeared puzzled. 'You don't seem surprised.'

'No, I am,' Merlin said hurriedly. 'It's a miracle!' It looked as if she was going to question him further, so he added: 'I could tell he must be well because you're smiling.'

The girl still stared at him. 'But you seemed to know already.'

Merlin froze for a second. He'd been so pleased with himself that he hadn't stopped to think, and he'd given himself away!

But of course Gwen couldn't really suspect that he had anything to do with the cure. He'd just have to make a joke of it and hope that would distract her; that she wouldn't think about it too much. 'Yeah, all right, you've finally found out,' Merlin said. 'I'll tell you. I'm psychic!'

She laughed. 'No you're not.'

'It's true!' Merlin protested.

'All right, what am I thinking?'

Merlin screwed up his face, like he was concentrating hard. 'That . . . I'm not psychic.'

Gwen laughed again, and Merlin smiled. She didn't suspect his secret. The danger had passed.

He had no idea how much danger there was still to come.

A crowd had gathered to see the miracle. Tom the blacksmith was hammering out a piece of metal on his anvil, as strong as he had ever been.

Word had reached Prince Arthur, and he pushed his way through the onlookers. 'The story is you were sick,' he said.

'Not any more,' Tom replied, grinning as he brought the hammer down again with a *thud*.

'Perhaps you were suffering from some

other ailment,' the prince suggested.

Tom shook his head. 'You're joking. I felt like death itself. Not enough strength in me to stir the air. Then suddenly – it was gone! And I'm fitter than I was before.'

Arthur looked incredulous. 'That's remarkable. Was anyone with you when this happened?'

'Just my daughter,' Tom told him. 'Gwen.'

The guards tore apart the blacksmith's house. And there, under Tom's pillow, they found a strange object. A tiny cloth-wrapped bundle that twinkled all on its own.

It was the poultice Merlin had made: it was obviously magical, and it was found in Gwen's house.

Minutes later, Gwen was under arrest – for sorcery.

Chapter Five

Condemned to Death

Gwen screamed as Arthur's guards dragged her away. Morgana, horrified, followed behind her maid.

Merlin heard the noise and rushed out of Gaius' chambers. Gwen saw him and cried out, 'Merlin! Please help me! I'm innocent!' He made to chase after her, but Gaius appeared at his side and dragged him back into the room.

The doctor slammed the door behind

them. 'What have you done?' he demanded furiously.

Merlin didn't answer. He was working out what must have happened, and the thought made him feel sick.

'Oh, I understand, you thought you were doing good,' said Gaius, and the anger on his face made Merlin feel even worse than he did already.

'I couldn't just let her father die, knowing I could cure him,' the boy protested.

'Did you not think it would look a bit suspicious, one man recovering, when the rest die?'

The truth was, Merlin hadn't thought any further than Gwen's happiness. He'd wanted to help his friend, and sorcery could do that – so it had seemed the right thing. 'Then all I have to do is . . . cure everyone!' he said desperately. 'No one will ever have to know it was magic.'

Gaius shook his head. 'It's too late. They think Gwen's a sorceress. They think she caused the disease.'

'But she didn't!'

'Oh, and how are you going to prove that?'

Merlin stared at the doctor as the full horror of the situation sank in. How *could* they prove that Gwen wasn't a sorcerer? And if they didn't – what would happen to her?

Gwen was on her hands and knees in front of the king. Tears were streaming down her cheeks. 'Why will no one believe me?' she cried. 'He got better. He just recovered. I didn't do anything!'

Arthur, watching, looked uncomfortable. Morgana, however, was furious. 'I believe you!' she announced. Her eyes blazed with fury as she stepped forward to address the king. 'Perhaps this is a disease that is not always fatal. Have you thought of that? Perhaps he recovered naturally.'

Merlin, sneaking into the room to watch, nodded eagerly. If only Uther could believe that – after all, the plague had only been in Camelot for a few days; they couldn't be expected to know everything about it already . . .

But his hopes were dashed – and horribly so. 'Then what of this poultice that was found?' Uther demanded.

Merlin's stomach turned to stone. How could he have forgotten about the poultice? He should have waited till Tom was up, then gone back to the house and removed it. But he'd never given it another thought. What an idiot he was! A magical object like that would prove Gwen's guilt – at least in Uther's blinkered eyes.

'I don't know anything about a poultice!'

Gwen protested.

'It was found in your house,' Uther said. 'Undo this enchantment, put an end to this disease!'

Gwen looked utterly hopeless. 'I can't.'

'Then I can show you no mercy.' The king held himself straight, staring down at the weeping girl as if she were no more than an animal. 'If you will not undo your sorcery, you force my hand and I must find you guilty. Under the circumstances, I have no choice but to sentence you to death.'

'No . . .' Gwen breathed.

'No!' Merlin echoed her horror. How could this be happening? How could anyone possibly believe that Gwen was capable of such evil acts? And it was all his fault!

Uther was still speaking, taking no notice of Gwen's exhausted protests. 'I can only hope that when you die, this evil plague

dies with you. Take her away!'

Gwen's eyes met Merlin's for an instant as the guards dragged her from the room. He wanted to say something; tell the king he'd got it all wrong; tell Gwen that he'd sort it all out . . . But before the thoughts had formed in his head, the girl was gone.

Now Morgana stepped forward again. 'I know Gwen,' she told Uther. 'She is my maidservant, not an enchantress.'

The king almost laughed. 'Have you ever seen an enchantress? Believe me, they bear no sign.'

'What I have seen is the way that girl works. Her fingers are worn, her nails are broken. If she were a sorceress, why would she do this? Why would she kneel on a cold stone floor morning after morning when she could make these things happen with the snap of her fingers' – Morgana clicked her fingers in demonstration – 'like an idle king.'

Uther turned on her. 'You have no right to comment.'

She wasn't cowed. 'Oh, but you have the right to cast a judgement!'

'I have the *responsibility* to protect the kingdom!' shouted the king. 'I take no pleasure in this.'

'But you are sentencing the wrong person,' Morgana cried.

Arthur stepped forward, slightly nervously. It was a dangerous business, questioning the king's wisdom. 'She's right, Father,' he said. Morgana turned to him in gratitude as he continued, 'You hear the word "magic" and you no longer listen.'

Uther obviously couldn't believe his ears. 'You saw it for yourself, she used enchantments.'

The prince didn't deny that. 'Yes, maybe

– but to save her dying father. That doesn't make her guilty of creating a plague. One's the act of kindness, of love . . . the other of evil. I don't believe evil is in this girl's heart.'

Merlin, listening, nodded violently. He hadn't realized how well Arthur knew Gwen – but of course, she had been maid to Morgana for years. The prince must have grown up with her, and no one who knew Gwen could doubt her goodness. If only the king would listen to his son's words.

'I've witnessed what witchcraft can do, I have suffered at its hands,' Uther said. 'I cannot take that chance. If there is the slightest doubt about this girl, she must die, or the whole kingdom may perish.'

Arthur nodded, placating his father. 'I understand that.'

The king was not to be patronized. 'One day you may become king: *then* you will understand. Such decisions *must* be made. There are dark forces that threaten this kingdom.'

'I know, witchcraft is an evil, Father,' Arthur replied. 'But, so is injustice! Yes, I am yet to be king. And I do not know what kind of king I will be.' He squared his shoulders, no longer nervous. 'But I do have a sense of the kind of Camelot I would wish to live in. It would be one where the punishment fits the crime.'

Merlin felt like cheering. Every time he started doubting Arthur, the prince did something like this that changed his mind. He'd be proud to be the subject of a king like that. He'd be prouder still to help put a king like that on the throne. Merlin even forgave Arthur for being the one who'd arrested Gwen in the first place – he hadn't had much choice, after all, once that poultice was found.

For a moment Merlin even thought that the prince's passion would soften Uther's heart.

Yet again, he was destined for disappointment.

'I fear you are right,' said the king. He stared straight at his son. 'The punishment *should* fit the crime. This girl played with fire – and sadly she must die by fire.'

CHAPTER SIX

MERLIN'S CONFESSION

Merlin could think of nothing except that he must see Gwen. Guilt and horror fought for dominance inside him. He wanted to confess to Gwen, tell her it was all his fault – but what would that achieve? She would go to her death hating him. Or, worse, knowing Gwen, she would forgive him – and how could he bear that?

He stood outside her cell now. She hadn't looked up at the sound of his steps; she was in a world far away. He winced as he saw the manacles that tethered her to the wall.

'Gwen . . .' he said gently.

After a moment she raised her eyes, and managed the smallest of smiles. 'Thank you.'

That almost broke Merlin's heart. 'What for?'

'For coming to see me.'

He couldn't smile back at her. 'I'm sorry.'

'It's not your fault,' she said.

It is, it is, it is! he screamed inside.

'It's all right. Don't worry about me. There's no point crying about it.' That hint of embarrassment was back again as she realized what she had said. 'I mean, I'm not saying you were going to cry about me. Obviously I don't think that . . .'

Merlin held out a hand through the bars, wishing he could reach her, wishing he could comfort her.

'Please. One thing,' she said. 'You don't have to . . . But . . .'

'What?' asked Merlin gently.

'Remember me.'

And now Merlin's heart really did break. The tears were starting to rise, but he pushed them back and let anger replace them. 'You're not going to die. I'm not going to let this happen.'

He ran from the dungeons, through the corridors, pushed past annoyed guards, until he was back outside Uther's council chambers. He wouldn't stop for a second, couldn't allow himself to think about what he was about to do. He burst through the doors.

An emergency meeting was in progress. Uther and Arthur were still there, and Gaius was standing at the head of the table. He was speaking as Merlin burst in – something about the need to cleanse the water supply – but he broke off in astonishment.

'It was me!' Merlin shouted. 'It was me who used magic to cure Gwen's father. Gwen is not the sorcerer – *I* am!'

Everyone stared at him. Gaius was the first to find words. 'Merlin! Are you mad?'

But Merlin knew he had never been saner. 'I cannot let her die for me,' he said simply. He turned to the king. 'I place myself at your mercy.'

'He doesn't know what he's talking

about,' Gaius said anxiously. 'I do!'

'Then arrest him,' the king said. His voice was cold and harsh.

Guards moved towards Merlin, but Arthur jumped to his feet, gesturing for them to hold back. 'Father, please. I can't allow this – it's madness. There's no way Merlin is a sorcerer.'

Uther would not be moved. 'He admitted it. Why should he fabricate such a story?'

Arthur stared at Merlin. Merlin stared back, willing the young man to believe him. All right, so it was nice of Arthur not to let his servant be arrested, but right now he'd prefer the prince to show his support by backing up Merlin's claim. Didn't he realize how much depended on it? Gwen's life was at stake!

But it was not to be. 'As Gaius said,' began Arthur after a moment, 'Merlin's got a grave mental disease.'

What? Merlin thought indignantly.

'He's in love.'

'What!' Now Merlin was indignant out loud.

'With Gwen,' Arthur continued.

'I am not!' cried Merlin. This couldn't be happening.

'I saw you yesterday with that flower she'd given you.'

That wasn't evidence! 'I'm not in love

with her,' Merlin said desperately. 'I don't even think of her like that!' What was Arthur *doing*? Gwen was just a friend – surely he knew that. Now the whole court was laughing at him.

Even *Uther* was laughing at him! 'Perhaps she cast a spell on you,' the king said.

Arthur waved a hand at his blushing servant. 'Merlin is a wonder. But the wonder is that he's such an idiot. There's no way he's a sorcerer.'

Merlin felt utterly frustrated. He couldn't work out if Arthur was doing his best to save his servant's life, or if the prince really thought of him like that. Should he be grateful or furious? And how come Uther wouldn't listen to his son when he pleaded for mercy for Gwen, but was happy to dismiss Merlin's genuine confession just because Arthur laughed at it? Perhaps if he actually cast a spell –

then they couldn't help but believe him!

But before Merlin had even thought of an incantation, he found himself bundled out of the room at the king's command.

Defeated, embarrassed and hopeless, he made his way back to Gaius' rooms.

CHAPTER SEVEN
THE AFANC

'*Arthur*'s the idiot,' said Merlin to Gaius later, still brooding on the prince's words.

'No, he was right to do what he did,' said Gaius. 'Thankfully he saved you from your own stupidity.'

Merlin shook his head. 'What else could I do? It's my fault that Gwen's going to die.'

'Yes,' the doctor agreed, 'but you don't prove her innocence by offering to jump into the flames. You do it by finding out what's causing the disease.' He passed Merlin a bag. 'Come on – we're going down to the vaults. We're going to find out what's contaminating the water supply.'

The door to the vaults was stiff, the latch rusty, but a brazier was burning inside from which Merlin lit a torch. They made their way down along twisted passages carved into the rock – if it wasn't for the burning torches on the walls, which must have been recently lit, Merlin would have thought they were the first people down here for years. It was cold and dank; a musty smell and eerie silence pervaded the atmosphere.

Eventually they came to a cave carved out of the stone, in which was a wide pool. All seemed calm; not a ripple disturbed the pool's surface. 'Take a sample,' Gaius instructed. 'The water from here supplies the whole city.'

Merlin passed his torch to Gaius and

leaned down to fill a small bottle. He put in the stopper and turned away, ready to start the long journey back through the tunnel . . .

When suddenly a huge monster leaped out of the water.

The two men yelled as they spun round, just in time to see the hideous creature vanish back under the surface. A second later, everything was still and silent again.

'What the hell was that?' Merlin whispered as they stumbled towards the door, desperate to get away. The young warlock just couldn't get the image out of his head – the monster looked like nothing he had ever seen, slimy and covered in clay-like globules, surely it

couldn't be of this earth.

'It was an Afanc,' said Gaius a little while later.

They were back in the doctor's chambers, leafing through a pile of old and dusty books. Gaius had just stopped at a page, pointing triumphantly at an illustration. Even though they had only glimpsed the creature briefly, Merlin had no difficulty in recognizing it. That terrifying instant was burned into his mind – the great grey hump-backed monster, all jaws and slime and talons.

'It's a beast born of clay,' Gaius continued. 'Conjured up only by the most powerful sorcerer.' He pushed the book aside and reached for another. 'Now we have to find a way to defeat it.'

Merlin shook his head. 'That could take days. Gwen will be dead by then.'

'Have you got a better idea?' Gaius asked.

Well, as a matter of fact – Merlin had.

In the caverns beneath the palace, far underground, a Dragon was imprisoned. When Uther had banished magic, twenty years before, he had had the Dragons slaughtered – all except one. The Great Dragon was kept as an example of the king's power over magic, and no one was permitted to see it.

But Merlin had heard the Dragon's call when he first arrived at Camelot, and he had responded. It was from the Dragon that he had learned of his destiny – that he would become a great warlock, and that with his aid Arthur would gain the throne.

Now he sought the Dragon's help for himself – and for Gwen, and for Camelot.

'Hello!' he shouted into the darkness.

After a moment the Dragon appeared, and Merlin suppressed a shiver of awe at the sight of the huge beast.

'The great warlock returns, as I knew he would,' it said.

Merlin didn't want to waste any time with this 'great warlock' business. 'I need to know how to defeat an Afanc.'

'Yes, I suppose you do.'

So the Dragon knew all about it. Merlin wasn't surprised: it seemed to know everything. 'Will you help me?' he asked it.

For a few moments there was silence. Merlin screamed inside with impatience. Every second brought them closer to Gwen's execution!

Finally the Dragon spoke. 'Trust the

elements that are at your command.'

'Elements? But what is it I have to do?' Merlin cried.

'You cannot do this alone,' said the Dragon. 'You are but one side of a coin; Arthur is the other.'

Now Merlin was close to screaming for real. Why did the Dragon always have to talk in riddles? Why did it always have to talk about coins and destiny and elements? Why couldn't it just say what

it meant? 'I don't understand,' he said.
'Just tell me what it is I have to do!'

The Dragon's huge black eyes stared
down at Merlin, who suddenly felt so
tiny. There might have been the hint of a
smile on its scaly jaws. Then its vast wings
unfurled and it swooped away.

'No!' Merlin shouted after it. 'Please, help
me!'

'I have . . .' a voice floated back.

'Yeah, right, thanks,' muttered Merlin as
the sound of the Dragon's laughter echoed
around him. Now he was going to have to
try to unravel the creature's riddle – and
time was running out.

Gwen's life depended on his finding an
answer, but he didn't even know where to
start looking.

CHAPTER EIGHT
TRUSTING THE ELEMENTS

'Merlin, what are you doing?' Gaius demanded, coming into his chambers to see Merlin rummaging through the contents of a bookcase.

'Looking for a book,' the boy replied. This was his brainwave. Well, the best idea he had come up with, anyway. Gaius had books on everything; if the answer was to be found anywhere, it would be here.

Gaius raised an eyebrow. 'Care to tell me which one?'

'A book on elements,' Merlin said. 'Which one would I find them in?'

'Well, most of them,' the doctor told him. 'The study of base elements is at the very heart of the scientific process. Earth, air, fire, water.'

Merlin turned away from the books. That reminded him of something. But what? Then he realized. 'Of course! The Afanc is a creature made from earth and water – that's two of the elements!' For a moment he felt really excited; then his hopes fell again. 'But how will that help me kill it?'

'Well . . .' Gaius thought for a second. 'That's earth and water. Maybe the other two elements would destroy it. Fire . . . and wind, perhaps.' He looked at his protégé in amazement. 'How did you think of this?'

Merlin certainly wasn't going to mention the Dragon. Gaius kicked up enough of a fuss when the boy cast a simple spell to clean shoes or something; he'd go crazy if he knew Merlin was breaking the law by visiting a magical creature more or less under the king's nose. 'Er . . . it's part of my powers,' he tried. 'I know I have to trust the elements that are at my command.'

Gaius didn't seem to buy this completely. 'What else do your powers tell you?' he asked suspiciously.

'That . . . I am only one side of a coin. The brighter side, obviously,' Merlin added.

'And who is the other side?'

Merlin smiled sheepishly. 'I think that may be Arthur.'

Luckily Merlin was saved from further questioning by the arrival of Morgana. The king's ward swept into the chambers. Even distraught, she made quite an entrance, and Merlin was struck – as he always was – by her incredible beauty. But he had no time to appreciate it:

the news she brought drove everything else from his mind.

'They're bringing forward the execution to tonight,' she told them. 'Uther has decided that too many people are dying, and he thinks this will stop the deaths. We have to prove Gwen's innocence.'

'We're trying,' Gaius said.

For a moment Merlin couldn't speak. It seemed as though every time he took a step nearer a solution, the king put another obstacle in his path.

Morgana looked past them both at the piles of books, the bubbling flasks, the half-completed experiments. 'Please, just tell me what I can do to help.'

And Merlin suddenly realized that something had actually gone right for a change. In bringing Morgana here, fate had dealt him the very card he needed. Merlin could never persuade the prince to help them, but Morgana would have no such problem. 'We need Arthur,' he told her.

She seemed surprised, and he knew he had to tell her everything. Well, almost everything. 'There's a monster, an Afanc, in the water supply. That's what's causing the plague.'

'Well, we must tell Uther!' she cried, half turning towards the door.

Gaius held out a hand to stop her. He gently shook his head. 'The Afanc's a creature forged by magic. Uther would just blame Gwen for conjuring it.'

'We need to destroy it, then the plague will stop,' Merlin continued. 'Then Uther may see sense. And Arthur's our best chance — but he won't want to disobey his father . . .'

Morgana had a determined glint in her eye, and Merlin knew he'd done exactly the right thing in telling her. 'Just leave that to me,' she said.

Arthur looked up and saw a sad-faced Morgana at the door of his room. Truth to tell, he didn't feel that happy himself. He didn't for a second believe that Gwen was an evil sorceress, but he knew he couldn't change his father's mind about executing her. He'd never been able to change his father's mind about anything. And it wasn't as if he had any ideas himself about how to stop this terrible disease.

'You all right?' he said. He saw Morgana looking past him at the dirty plates, the half-eaten food and scattered clothes, and grimaced. 'I'm sorry about all this. Merlin's not been in today.'

'Poor Merlin,' said Morgana. 'To offer to give up his life for Gwen's. I certainly can't imagine any man loving me so much.'

She was staring hard at him as she spoke, and Arthur couldn't hold back a sarcastic reply. 'No, I certainly can't imagine that either.' This always happened with Morgana! He tried to be nice, but she just . . . wound him up! When she wasn't around, he thought quite fondly of her. But as soon as she appeared in person, all his good resolutions fell away.

Morgana smiled now, mocking him. 'That's because you're not like Merlin. He's a lover.'

'Yeah, maybe that's because I haven't found the right person to love.' The idea that anyone could think that his servant – nice enough lad though Merlin was – was better than him, was frankly ridiculous.

And that gave him the clue. Clearly Morgana was just saying all this for effect – she couldn't possibly mean it; she was just trying to get a response. Her next words made that very clear.

She sighed dramatically. 'Sadly, the age of gallantry seems to be dead. You look around – and all you see is small men, not big enough to fill their armour. There's not one of them who is able to stand up for what is right.'

He tried not to laugh at such obvious tactics. But, well, if she was trying this hard, it had to be something important. 'What do you want me to do?' he asked.

Merlin was amazed but happy when Morgana turned up a short time later with Arthur at her side. The prince had a sword at his belt and a torch in his hand, ready to enter the palace vaults. At last things were going to plan!

Together, the warlock, the prince and the king's ward made their way down into the depths of the palace, then crept along the dank tunnels that led towards the pool. Arthur and Morgana both carried torches; the flames dancing wickedly on the uneven

walls reminded Merlin uncomfortably of the fate that awaited Gwen if they failed in their task.

'You should stay here,' Arthur said to Morgana as they reached the entrance to the cold and silent cave.

Merlin could have told him he might as well have saved his breath. Morgana obeyed no man, and she was as brave as any Dragon. 'Scared I'll show you up?' she said.

'Father would slam us both in chains if he knew I'd endangered you,' he retorted.

She grinned. 'Good thing he doesn't know about it, then.' She pushed past the prince and entered the cave. Arthur drew his sword as he followed. Merlin was pleased about that. He didn't feel anywhere near as brave as Morgana – but then, he'd seen the Afanc before and she hadn't.

'Stop!' Arthur called suddenly. Merlin froze. Was that something moving in the shadows? He was *trying* to be brave – they had to do this, for Gwen. But his mind kept having to tell his body not to run away. They had to find the monster – that was

the whole point of coming down here —
but Merlin really, really didn't want to see
it again.

After a moment Arthur shook his head.
Merlin breathed a sigh of relief, and they
carried on.

The prince told them to spread out.
This, Merlin thought, was a very bad idea.
Arthur obviously thought that they'd be
more likely to find the monster like that.
What he seemed to have failed to consider
was that it would also be more likely for
the monster to find them — and much,
much easier for it to deal with them one
at a time. Could it be that Arthur didn't
feel afraid at all? He didn't look it. The
prince was fond of telling people that
he'd been trained to kill since birth — but
Merlin doubted that the training included
giant supernatural monsters.

Reluctantly the young warlock headed

off to one side; Morgana went the other way. Merlin was hardly breathing now. Surely the Afanc could hear every beat of his heart! Surely it was tracking him down, getting ready to strike . . .

'*Aargh!*' Suddenly there was a yell from Arthur, and Merlin nearly jumped out of his skin. He rushed back towards the prince, just in time to get an impression of something monstrous sinking back into the water − something huge with slimy, globulous skin.

'Did you see it?' he asked anxiously.

Arthur nodded. 'It's quick,' he said, shuddering at the thought of the monster towering over him only seconds before.

Merlin was still scared, but suddenly it was as though a great weight had been lifted from him. It wasn't just relief that Arthur was unhurt − it was the realization that he didn't seem a bit surprised that they'd actually found the monster. After all the things that had happened before, this time he hadn't doubted Merlin, hadn't been humouring him. He'd believed him without question, and that suddenly meant an awful lot.

Then Morgana screamed. Merlin, jerked out of his thoughts, spun round in horror – there was the Afanc, bearing down on her! Its huge cavernous mouth opened in a terrible roar. Arthur leaped forward with his sword – and the creature was gone again.

The three stood rooted to the spot. No one could believe that a beast that size could move so swiftly or so silently – and no one knew where it might appear next. They stared around nervously.

Again, Merlin thought he caught a glimpse of something moving in the shadows. 'I think it's gone this way,' he called, astonished to find that his voice wasn't trembling.

And suddenly there it was, above him. In an instant Arthur was at his side, sword raised. He swung at the monster, but the blade just glanced off its skin, the clay harder than rock.

In alarm, the prince thrust his flaming torch at the beast. It shied away, but only for a moment, then its talons swiped down again, this time missing Arthur by inches.

But it had been scared of the torch: Merlin had seen that. The flaming torch – fire. Wielded by Arthur. To solve the Dragon's riddle, the last element was needed to complete the set – wind.

Suddenly Merlin no longer felt afraid. Magic filled him, and left no room for fear. A heat rose up inside him, and as the power flared, his eyes glowed as bright as any fire.

'Arthur, use the torch!' he cried.

Desperately the prince lunged forward. Merlin's eyes shone with a golden light as a wind sprang up in the cavern – a magical wind. The flames from the torch were picked up by the wind; they grew huge and

billowed through the cave. The Afanc was engulfed in fire, and Merlin, Arthur and Morgana watched in fear and wonder as it was destroyed.

The creature's dying roar echoed around another cave, many miles away. Nimueh watched her creation fall to the ground; then her fist punched the surface of the scrying pool, shattering the image. She screamed in anger. '*Merlin!*'

CHAPTER NINE
THE MARK OF NIMUEH

'Good news, sire. There are no new deaths, and those that are sick are recovering.'

Gaius smiled as he passed on the good news to the king, and Uther smiled in return. 'Good.' He thought for a moment. 'Strange, I've never heard of an Afanc before.'

'It's conjured from clay by powerful magic,' the physician told him. 'The type that can only be invoked by an ancient

sorcerer. One who has the power to mirror the spirit of life.'

The king looked horror-struck as Gaius produced a piece of eggshell that had held the growing Afanc. It was covered in strange markings.

'I went down to the water source after the monster was destroyed, and I found this.' He paused, obviously realizing the impact his next words would have. 'It bears the mark of Nimueh.'

'No . . .' whispered Uther. 'Will I never be rid of her . . . ?' Then he turned away. 'Leave me!' he shouted. 'Leave me!'

Gaius hurried out.

If Nimueh had still

been watching, she would have found some consolation in the sight. Her plan might have failed – but there was no question that she had brought terror and fear to the king she so hated.

Merlin couldn't stop grinning. The Afanc was dead. Amazingly, neither Arthur nor Morgana had realized that the whirlwind in the cave came from him; they seemed to assume that it was the magical nature of the monster itself that had caused the flames to swallow it. Once again, of course, that meant Merlin got no recognition for his amazing feat – but he was learning to cope with that. And anyway, nothing could take the shine off this morning, because here they were, watching Gwen being released from prison. He felt almost giddy with relief. Somehow they'd managed to turn everything around – not only repairing the harm that his magic had caused, but ridding Camelot of the sickness too.

The girl rushed out of the cell into the arms of her father, Tom, who swung her round in joy. Merlin still felt guilty for what had happened to Gwen, but looking at her happiness now, he found it hard to regret saving her father. He knew he had to consider the consequences of his actions more carefully, but he honestly wasn't sure that he wouldn't do exactly the same thing again.

When father and daughter could finally tear their delighted eyes away from each other, Gwen spotted Merlin and Morgana watching. She hurried over. 'Thank you,' she said breathlessly.

'Don't thank me,' said Morgana. 'It was more Merlin.'

Merlin tried not to be offended that Gwen seemed to find this hard to believe.

'Really?' she asked.

'He's the real hero here,' Morgana insisted.

'Oh, I didn't do anything,' Merlin said unconvincingly.

Gwen beamed at him. 'I don't know what to say.'

Tom put his arm around her shoulders. 'I'm grateful to you all. Come on, Gwen.' He led her away.

Merlin happily watched them go. Well, a little bit of recognition was a nice thing.

'Merlin, I wanted you to know . . .' Morgana interrupted his thoughts. 'Your secret's safe with me.'

'My secret?' Merlin's heart leaped. So – so she had realized! She had seen him defeat the Afanc – and she was smiling; she

wasn't going to tell Uther; instead she would become his ally! Could the day get any better?

'I saw it with my own eyes,' she said. 'But I understand why you don't want anyone to know.'

'Well, obviously . . .' Merlin agreed.

'And I won't tell anyone. You don't mind me talking to you about it, though?'

Mind! Merlin had never felt happier. 'Oh no – you have no idea how hard it is to keep this hidden.'

Morgana nodded. 'Well, you can continue to deny it, but . . . I think Gwen's a very lucky woman.'

What? She didn't know about his magic at all – she thought he was in love with Gwen!

She raised a finger to her lips. 'It's our secret.'

Merlin sighed ruefully as she left, all thoughts of talking about magic with Morgana disappearing even quicker than they'd arrived.

'No one seems to appreciate my skills,' he moaned later to Gaius, wondering if anyone would ever realize how much he and his magic had done for Camelot.

The elderly doctor looked concerned. 'I hope they don't,' he said. 'This was all the work of a very powerful sorcerer. We have to trust that you haven't come to her attention.'

'I just want someone to see me for who I am,' Merlin grumbled.

'One day, Merlin . . .' Gaius said.

'One day what?'

The old man put an arm around the boy.

'One day people won't believe what an idiot you were.'

They smiled at each other. Neither suspected that Gaius' words were a foreshadowing of what was to come. Because in her deep, dark cave, Nimueh was already making new plans.

Plans for Merlin.

CHAPTER TEN
THE GOBLET

It was not many days before Nimueh came up with a new plan, though it took several weeks of preparation to put it into action. First she travelled to the court of Lord Bayard of Mercia, where she adopted the name Kara and took a job as a servant, ensuring that her pretty face and pleasing manners brought her to the attention of Bayard's wife, Margaret. Then she used a sleeping draught on one of Margaret's handmaidens: the girl was dismissed for oversleeping and not attending to her duties. Nimueh was careful to be nearby at the time with offers of help, and she was soon given the poor girl's job. She pretended to be surprised to hear that Bayard and Margaret would soon be travelling to Camelot – and that, as Margaret's handmaiden, she would be required to go too.

Of course, Nimueh had known about this all along. In her scrying bowl she had watched the messengers riding back and forth between Uther and Bayard, agreeing the terms of a treaty – for the kingdoms of Camelot and Mercia had been fighting for many years. She had decided that being part of the Mercian court would be the perfect way to get close to Uther without anyone suspecting a thing – because every eye would be on Bayard, not his servants.

In her scrying bowl, she had seen the

peace gift that Bayard planned to take to Camelot's king – a pair of goblets, crafted by Mercia's finest silversmith. The rest of her plan suddenly fell into place.

As Mercia's knights and nobles began the long ride to Camelot, none suspected that in the saddlebags of Margaret's pretty new servant a third goblet could be found. A duplicate, created with great magical skill, that would soon replace one of the genuine cups. And in the base of this goblet lay a single translucent petal.

'Why do I always get landed with the donkey work?' Merlin grumbled as he staggered past Gaius with a load of Mercian knights' luggage in his arms.

'You're a servant, Merlin; it's what you do,' the doctor reminded him.

This failed to cheer up Merlin, who thought of himself as a warlock who just did a bit of servanting on the side. He was just opening his mouth to tell Gaius exactly what he thought of it, when a pile of bedding fell at his feet. He turned to the person who was bending down to pick it up.

Merlin's mouth stayed open, and his jaw dropped further. The servant who was crouched down in front of him was quite the loveliest girl he had ever seen, with the brightest blue eyes. 'I'm sorry . . .' she began.

'Let me give you a hand with that,' Merlin said hurriedly, bending down to help her collect the spilled cushions and sheets. 'Hi. I'm Merlin.'

'Kara,' she said as they both stood up again. 'You're Arthur's servant, aren't you? That must be such an honour.'

Merlin was even prepared to admit to serving Arthur if it impressed this amazing-looking girl. 'Oh yeah, it is. Well,' he added, 'someone's got to keep the place running.'

She smiled at the joke and took back the cushion he hadn't realized he was still holding. 'Well, it was nice meeting you,' she said, and walked off.

Gaius watched in disapproval as Merlin gazed after the girl. 'Shouldn't you be busy "running the place"?' he commented.

With a grin, Merlin hurried off. Why

moan about being a servant when it brought you into contact with such interesting people . . . ?

There was a banquet that evening in honour of the signing of the peace treaty. Merlin was there to wait on Arthur. He was hoping to see Kara again – although part of him was hoping that she wouldn't see him, dressed as he was in ceremonial robes complete with an embarrassingly large and feathered hat. Arthur had insisted that it was what all the servants would be wearing, but this turned out not to be the case. Merlin strongly suspected that the prince was playing a joke at his expense.

He wasn't really all that bothered, though, despite the embarrassment. A bond had developed between Merlin and Arthur after all they'd been through, and if that included a few practical jokes along the way, well, that's just the way Arthur was.

'Nice hat,' commented Gwen with a smile. She was attending Morgana, and was her usual sunny self. No one could have guessed that she had recently been through such a terrible ordeal. Merlin wondered how she could bear to be in the same room as the king, who had sentenced her to death only weeks before. But of course, that was all part of being a servant. You had little choice about where you went or what you did or who you saw, and you had to be happy – or at least *look* happy – with it all.

This only strengthened Merlin's belief that he was not natural servant material.

But then he glanced over at Prince Arthur, desperately trying to look polite as he was introduced to yet another noble of Mercia, and realized that princes had little choice about where they went or what they did or who they saw either; they just had nicer food and didn't have to wear silly hats.

His eyes searched the crowd of Mercian servants, and found Kara. Hurriedly he removed the hat, just in case she happened to look in his direction. Gwen followed his gaze. 'She's pretty, isn't she?' she said. 'For a handmaiden, I mean . . .'

'She's pretty for a princess, let alone a handmaiden,' Merlin said, not taking his eyes off her for a second.

CHAPTER ELEVEN
POISONED!

Kara seemed very interested in a wooden box that lay in the arms of one of the Mercian servants. Merlin wondered what it held. Perhaps he would find out soon, for the servant stepped forward when Bayard rose to give a speech.

'People of Camelot,' Bayard began. 'For a great many years we have been mortal enemies. The blood of our men stains the ground from the walls of Camelot to the gates of Mercia, and though we remember those who have died, we must not allow any more to join them. As a symbol of our goodwill and of our new-found friendship, I present these ceremonial goblets to you, Uther, and to your son, Arthur, in the hope that our friendship may last.'

The wooden box was brought to Bayard. He took from it two silver goblets, and handed one to the king and one to his son. A servant came forward to fill them with wine.

Merlin had been distracted by the speech and the box. He hadn't noticed Kara moving across the room, so he was surprised to realize she was by his side. He was pleased – until he noticed her expression. She looked terrified. 'Merlin, I need to speak to you,' she whispered urgently. 'Please – I don't know who else to tell.'

He followed her from the room. She led him to a doorway, out of the way of the servants hurrying to and fro with food and wine, and began to speak. She talked so quickly and quietly that Merlin had to bend his head to hear her. 'It wasn't until I saw him give the goblet to Arthur that I realized . . .'

'Slow down,' he said. 'Start from the beginning.'

She took a deep breath. 'Two days ago I was bringing Bayard his evening meal. We're supposed to knock – he didn't expect me to walk in . . . Oh, if he knows I've said anything he'll kill me!'

'I will not let that happen to you, I promise,' Merlin said, hoping he'd be able to keep his word. But he had to know what she'd witnessed. 'Please, tell me what you saw.'

'Bayard is no friend to Camelot!' The girl looked at him, her bright blue eyes wide and scared. 'He craves the kingdom

for himself. He believes that if he kills Arthur, Uther's spirit will be broken and Camelot will fall. I saw him putting poison in Arthur's goblet!'

The final words had barely left her mouth when Merlin ran off, back to the banqueting hall. Arthur was in danger!

If the boy had glanced back, he would have been very surprised to see the ugly look of triumph on the face of the pretty maidservant.

Would he be in time? Would he be in time? Why hadn't she said anything earlier? Merlin burst through the doors.

'To your health, Uther, Arthur, the Lady Morgana, the people of Camelot,' said Bayard.

'And to fallen warriors on both sides,' Uther added.

Bayard raised his goblet in a toast. Uther and Arthur joined him. Arthur lifted his goblet to his mouth—

'Stop! It's poisoned! Don't drink it!' Merlin cried.

Everyone turned in amazement to look at the servant boy.

'Merlin, what are you doing?' asked Arthur, frowning.

Merlin turned to the king. 'Bayard laced

Arthur's goblet with poison,' he said.

There was a *shting!* as Bayard's sword left its scabbard. 'This is an outrage!' he cried, holding the sword in front of him – but a dozen other blades were pointing back. Uther's guards had stepped forward, surrounding the king's guests.

Uther looked furious. 'On what grounds do you base this accusation?' he growled at Merlin.

The young warlock glanced around the room. There were drawn swords everywhere. But he had to tell them what he knew. He couldn't risk Arthur being poisoned, even if it meant war.

'He was seen lacing it,' he said.

'By whom?' demanded Uther.

It took all Merlin's courage to keep quiet in the face of Uther's anger: he knew that the less information he gave the king, the less likely it was he'd be believed. He had to

save Arthur – but he'd promised Kara that he'd keep her name out of it. Her life was at risk – perhaps as much as the prince's.

The king stared at Merlin for a moment, and then turned to Arthur. 'Pass me the goblet.' He took it – and walked over to Bayard. 'If you're innocent,' he said, looking his one-time enemy in the eye, 'then you have nothing to fear, have you?' He held out the cup.

Bayard made to take it, his expression proud and angry – but at the last second Uther pulled it back. 'No. If this does prove to be poisoned, I want the pleasure of killing you myself.' He turned to Merlin. '*He'll* drink it.'

Merlin suddenly found himself holding the goblet. The wine inside shimmered in the candlelight.

Arthur stood up. 'But if it's poisoned, he'll die!' he cried. Merlin thought he actually sounded really worried, which was sort of nice. He didn't mind someone making him wear a silly hat so much if they'd also stand up for him like this. Not that Uther was likely to take any notice of his son.

And of course Uther didn't. 'Then we'll know he was telling the truth,' was all the king said.

Bayard stared at Merlin with hatred. 'And what if he lives?'

'Then you'll have my apologies,' Uther told him, 'and you can do with him what you will.'

Arthur leaned forward. 'Merlin, apologize.' He turned to his father again. 'This is a mistake. I'll drink it.'

But Merlin couldn't let that happen. 'No, it's all right,' he said. He felt sad inside – sad that the end had come so suddenly and unexpectedly, but he couldn't let himself think about that. He just had to save Arthur. As his destiny said he must.

Gwen took a step forward, as if to try and stop him.

He raised the goblet to his lips and drank.

Nothing happened.

Merlin stared down at the empty cup, confused. Had Kara

been mistaken? Oh well. He would probably be executed now anyway, but at least there wouldn't be a war as well.

'It's fine,' he said.

Uther turned to Bayard. 'He's all yours.'

Bayard and his knights moved towards Merlin.

But the boy suddenly found he couldn't breathe. Was this fear? No

– he *really* couldn't breathe ... He clutched at his throat, trying to draw in air, trying to say what was happening to him, but the world was turning grey around him.

Merlin fell to the floor. As people swarmed towards him, the goblet dropped from his limp hand and rolled away.

CHAPTER TWELVE
ARTHUR'S CHOICE

Uther's guards closed in on Bayard and his men. But Arthur's thoughts weren't on matters of state; they were on the unconscious boy at his feet. The boy who had saved his life. He picked up Merlin and hurried off to Gaius' chambers. A horrified Gwen snatched up the fallen goblet and followed.

When he saw them, Gaius' face was grim. 'Lay him on the bed quickly,' he said, pointing at his own pallet on the floor.

'And Gwen, fetch me some water and a towel.'

'Is he going to be all right?' asked Arthur anxiously as Gaius started to examine Merlin.

'You can cure him, can't you?' Gwen put in.

But the doctor had no reassuring words for either of them. 'I won't know until I can identify the poison,' he said.

Gaius picked up the goblet and moved over to his workbench, leaving Gwen bathing Merlin's forehead in cool water. A few seconds later he gave an exclamation. 'There's something stuck to the inside,' he said. Using a pair of tweezers, he pulled out a tiny flower petal. He examined it for a moment, and then moved over to a bookcase.

'What is it? Is Merlin going to die?' Arthur asked.

Gaius turned over the pages of a book, looking very grave. He found what he was looking for and read carefully for a few minutes, then addressed Arthur and Gwen.

'The petal is from the Mortaeus flower. It says here that someone poisoned by the Mortaeus can only be saved by a potion made from the leaf of the very same flower, which grows on the roots of the Mortaeus tree. It can only be found in the caves deep beneath the forest of Balor.' And there was worse to come. 'The forest is guarded by the Cockatrice. Its venom is potent. A single drop would mean certain death. Few who have crossed the mountains of Isgard in search of the Mortaeus flower have made it back alive.'

'Sounds like fun,' said Arthur, rubbing his hands together purposefully.

Gaius shook his head. 'Arthur, it's too dangerous.'

'If I don't get the antidote, what happens to Merlin?'

The doctor answered reluctantly, 'The Mortaeus induces a slow and painful death. He may hold out for four, maybe five days, but not for much longer. Eventually he will die.'

It all seemed very clear to Arthur. Merlin had risked the king's wrath to warn his prince of the danger, then willingly drunk the poison meant for him. Arthur had been brought up by the knight's code, and he respected noble and brave deeds. This, to him, was one of the bravest, noblest deeds he'd ever witnessed, and Merlin didn't deserve to die for it.

It was Arthur's duty to do whatever he could to save Merlin in return. It would be his duty even if he hadn't come to . . . well, to *like* his servant. He'd never *tell* Merlin that, of course. It wouldn't do. But there was a connection between them. Servants had always been like part of the furniture, hovering discreetly in the background and doing chores when needed — but Arthur actually enjoyed Merlin's company.

So Merlin didn't deserve to die — and Arthur didn't *want* him to die. There was no question, then, that the prince must act to save his servant.

Uther, however, did not see things in quite the same way.

'You're my only son and heir. I can't risk losing you for the sake of some serving boy,' the king told him, confronting the prince as he was about to leave the palace.

'Because his life's worthless?' Arthur said.

'No, because it's worth less than yours.' There was no sympathy on Uther's face. 'One day I will be dead and Camelot will need a king. I can't let you jeopardize this kingdom's future over some fool's errand.'

Arthur was disappointed that his father showed so little faith in him; thought him unable to overcome the slightest peril. But that wasn't an argument he wanted to get into now. What he needed Uther to understand was that Merlin had to be cured. 'Please, Father . . . he saved my life,' Arthur said. 'I can't stand by and watch him die.'

'Then don't look.' The king's voice was harsh. 'This boy won't be the last to die on your behalf. You're going to be king: it's something you'll have to get used to.'

'I can't accept that,' Arthur told him. The idea appalled him. There had to be a way to rule without leaving bodies strewn in his wake. There and then he decided that his reign would never be like that. 'You can't stop me going,' he said.

'Damn it, Arthur!' the king roared. 'You're not leaving this castle tonight!'

A fuming and frustrated Arthur stormed back to his own rooms. He shouldn't feel surprised. He'd never been able to change his father's mind before; why should this time be different? But although every instinct he possessed was urging him to defy the king and rescue Merlin, he was forced to admit that there was a grain of truth in Uther's unwelcome words. Camelot had no other heir. If Arthur was killed, the kingdom could be plunged into chaos.

And yet Uther was willing to see his son risk his life in combat. Arthur thought back to a recent tournament. The king had thought him a coward when he accused a fellow knight of cheating, then sat and watched while Arthur fought the man, who was trying to kill him with magic. It was Merlin who had warned the prince of the danger then.

He was pacing the room, his head in a whirl, when there was a knock at the door. Morgana came in.

'Back so soon?' she said. 'I'd heard you were off across the mountains of Isgard.' She paused. 'I suppose Uther heard the same thing.'

Arthur nodded. He sat down on the bed, his head in his hands. 'The thing is, if I don't make it back, who'll be the next king of Camelot? There's more than just my life at stake, you see.'

Morgana picked up Arthur's discarded sword and drew it from its scabbard. 'What kind of king would Camelot want? One who would risk his life to save that of a lowly servant – or one who does what his father tells him to?'

She held out the sword to Arthur. He
paused for a moment, but he could tell
Morgana wasn't sneering at him as she
sometimes did. She was helping him to see
things more clearly. If he didn't do what he
knew to be right, then he didn't deserve to
rule. An unworthy king, one who stayed at
home whenever danger threatened, would
be no use to the kingdom – so rescuing
Merlin was best for everyone. What his
instincts – what his *heart* was telling him to
do was the right thing.

He took the sword.

The guards at the gate weren't expecting
any trouble. Bayard and his party were

WHAT KIND OF KING WOULD CAMELOT WANT?

all locked in the dungeons, and no one with any sense would stir from his bed on such a dark, cold night. So they were taken completely by surprise when a horse galloped towards them from the direction of the castle. Before they had time to react, horse and rider were through and heading off into the distance – but they recognized the crest on the rider's armour, and wondered why Prince Arthur would be so eager to leave Camelot in the middle of the night.

CHAPTER THIRTEEN
GAIUS REALIZES

Gwen hadn't left Merlin's side all night. Now, as she bathed his forehead, the boy started to mumble beneath his breath. She leaned nearer to try to make out his words.

'*Liffrea, wuldres wealdend, woroldare forgeaf,*' Merlin muttered.

'What language is that?' Gwen called to Gaius.

The doctor realized what Merlin was saying, and hurried over. 'The fever's taken hold,' he told her quickly, hoping desperately that whatever spells Merlin was murmuring would have no visible effects. 'None of those words are his own.' He took hold of the boy's wrist, feeling for his pulse. 'It's getting weaker,' he said. Then he noticed something that had not been there before.

On Merlin's arm, a purple-ringed rash had appeared.

'What is it?' Gwen asked.

Gaius frowned. 'The rash isn't supposed to appear until the final stage.'

'What does that mean?' said Gwen.

He held up a hand to stop further questions as he went to consult his books; he returned a few minutes later carrying a volume about poisons. 'According to this, once the rash appears, death will follow within two days.'

Gwen was horrified. 'You said he had four days!'

'Something's increased the flower's potency.' Gaius began to leaf hurriedly through the book. 'It says that the effect of the Mortaeus will be more rapid if an enchantment is used during the flower's preparation.'

'But Bayard's no sorcerer!' Gwen cried.

'No,' agreed Gaius, shaking his head. 'No, he isn't.' He stared down at the still figure on the bed. Could it really have been only the day before that he'd been watching Merlin, full of life, flirting with one of Bayard's servants – the girl with the piercing blue eyes . . . ? And then – yes, Merlin had been seen talking to a Mercian maidservant just before he denounced Bayard!

'What happened to that girl?' he demanded of Gwen. 'The serving girl who took Merlin outside the hall. Do you know the one I mean?'

Gwen nodded. 'She had dark hair – very beautiful.'

'Find her. Quickly!'

She leaped up and ran out of the room. Gaius put his head in his hands. 'It can't be . . . She wouldn't dare come here . . .'

But he knew that his suspicions would

turn out to be correct. It was no matter that the girl looked nothing like the wom-

ARTHUR HAS GONE!

an he'd once known; he was aware that the most powerful sorcerers could enchant the eye that beheld them. The beautiful young maidservant was not beautiful or young or a maidservant, and he knew that her name was not Kara, as she had claimed.

Her name was Nimueh, and Gaius was certain that Gwen would never find her.

'I expressly ordered Arthur not to go!' Uther yelled.

The luckless guard who had just informed the king that his son had left during the night made a swift exit.

'I can see it worked like a charm too,' said Morgana calmly.

Uther glared at her. 'Not another word.' He clenched his fists. 'I should have put him under lock and key.'

'You can't chain him up every time he disagrees with you.'

'Just you watch me.' The king thumped the breakfast table. 'You knew about this, didn't you, Morgana?'

She didn't answer.

'Don't lie to me.'

Morgana gazed defiantly at her guardian. 'Arthur's old enough to make decisions for himself.'

The king shook his head. 'He's just a boy ...'

'Have you seen your son recently?' she said. 'You have to let him make up his own mind.'

Uther stared her straight in the eye. 'Even if it means letting him go to his death?'

Gwen had returned to Merlin's bedside, her search for the girl proving fruitless – as Gaius had known it would. The sorceress would have left the castle as soon as she'd put her plan into action.

'Who is she really?' Gwen asked the physician. 'You know, don't you?'

He couldn't tell her everything he knew. 'A powerful sorceress,' was all he said. Uther had forbidden him to speak of Nimueh; forbidden him to mention the time long ago when they had first met. No one must know why she hated Uther so much – why she would want to kill the king's only son and bring him so much pain. 'Oh no . . .' A sudden, terrible thought had struck him.

'What?' Gwen asked.

'She knows the only place an antidote can be found is the forest of Balor. Arthur could be walking into a trap!'

CHAPTER FOURTEEN
THE FOREST OF BALOR

Arthur was leading his horse through the dense forest. Neither had stopped since leaving Camelot and he needed to give the animal a rest – even if he couldn't afford to stop for a proper break.

The trees began to thin out, and soon they reached a clearing. To Arthur's astonishment, a young woman sat there, weeping. If he had paid more attention to Bayard's servants, he might have recognized her as the one who had disappeared with

Merlin just before the boy had accused Bayard of poisoning the goblet. But he hadn't noticed her in the castle, and now he simply wondered what the girl could be doing in such a dangerous place.

The prince called out a greeting and she turned – and screamed. Arthur spun round and found a huge monster bearing down on him – a great lizard with vast, sail-like fins on its back. He recognized it as the Cockatrice from Gaius' book.

In a flash Arthur's sword was in his hand, but the beast moved quickly and slid away from the blows. It was in the clearing now, and Arthur hurried to place himself between the monster and the terrified girl. The creature reared again, and lunged forward. Arthur ducked and dived underneath it. Perhaps he should have felt scared, but he was too exhilarated. It felt good to be having a real battle again after

weeks of the pretend fights in the training ground. Still, he didn't want to engage the monster in close combat; Gaius' warnings about its venom rang in his ears. As the creature turned, wondering where its prey had gone, the prince raised his sword — and threw. The blade tumbled through the air, end over end, and buried itself in the beast's heart. It fell to the ground and lay still.

The prince retrieved his sword and wiped it clean.

The young girl cowered

away as he approached, but he held out a hand. 'It's all right. I'm not going to hurt you.' She was covered in welts and bruises. To Arthur, she looked like a timid girl who had been cruelly mistreated, and he felt a surge of hatred towards the villain who had hurt her like this. He had no way of knowing that the weals were created by a magical illusion.

'Please don't leave me!' she cried, staring at him with wide blue eyes. 'I ran away from my master, but then I got lost. Can you take me away from here?'

Arthur shook his head. She was in no immediate danger, and he wasn't going to let even beauty in distress distract him from his mission. He'd seen a cave entrance on the other side of the clearing, and that was what he'd been searching for.

'There's something I have to do first,' he told her. 'I'm looking for something that can only be found here.'

She smiled at him. 'I know this place – I could help you. What are you looking for?'

'It's a type of flower that only grows inside the cave,' he explained. 'It's very rare.'

To the prince's surprise, she immediately said: 'The Mortaeus flower?' He nodded. 'I know where they are. I'll show you.'

And as Arthur reflected on his luck in meeting this girl, Nimueh took his arm and led him into the cave.

Many miles away, Merlin suddenly began tossing and turning on his bed. Gaius and Gwen bent over him in concern.

'Arthur . . . it's a trap . . . it's a trap,'

the boy muttered.

Gwen looked at the physician. 'His fever's getting worse, isn't it?' She tried not to show just how upset she was, but Gaius wasn't fooled. He had no words of comfort for her, though.

'Yes. The poison's setting in.' A string of strange syllables fell from the boy's lips, and Gaius recognized once again the incantation of a spell. 'Will you fetch me some more wolfbane?' he asked Gwen, partly to give her something to do and partly to distract her from Merlin's magical words.

She nodded and hurried off.

Gaius anxiously mopped the boy's fevered brow. 'Merlin, you must fight it,' he pleaded. If only he could hold out until Arthur returned . . .

Arthur had brought torches with him –

one of which he handed to the girl – and he was thankful for his foresight as they walked deeper and deeper into the gloomy caves. As she led him round a corner, Arthur suddenly came to a standstill. The path had ended, and in front of them lay a vast, dark chasm.

The girl pointed ahead, to the far side of the cave. 'There they are.' The prince held his torch out in front of him, but the strange plant was so high on the cave wall that he could barely see it.

He crept carefully forward, and threw a stone over the edge of the abyss. It vanished into the gloom, and they never heard it hit the bottom – the rift was very deep. Arthur wondered how he would ever get across – then he spotted an outcrop of rock that stretched out across the gulf. Could it possibly take his weight?

He thought of Merlin on his sick bed –

and he considered how scornful Morgana would be if he gave up and went back now. He had no choice other than to try it. 'Keep back,' he told the girl as he began to inch his way out towards the far side.

He was halfway across when the rock suddenly heaved beneath his feet. He looked back, and saw the girl standing there, her voice raised in command, her hand pointing at the outcrop.

'What are you doing?' he cried.

She only laughed and chanted louder. Arthur couldn't believe the transformation. This was no frightened girl: she was looking at him with a mixture of disdain and triumph. He cursed himself for being fooled; for being so easily taken in by a pretty face and a few tears. Perhaps his father was right to doubt him.

The torch fell from Arthur's hand as the rock shook again. He ran as fast as he could

towards the far side of the chasm, the rock collapsing under him. With a desperate last effort he jumped – and somehow his fingers caught hold of a protruding ledge.

Hanging in the darkness, he looked over his shoulder at the witch who had caused all this. She stepped forward, the torchlight illuminating her cruel smile. 'I expected so much more from you,' she told him.

Arthur struggled to maintain his grip. She was talking as if she knew him – surely she must at least explain why she wanted him dead? 'Who are you?' he demanded. But his curiosity was not to be satisfied.

'The last face you'll ever see.' She glanced

above him. 'It seems we have a visitor.'

Arthur followed her gaze. A giant spider was scuttling along the ledge towards his rigid fingers.

Summoning all his strength, the prince let go of the rock with one hand, and drew his sword. Desperately trying to keep his balance, he swept the blade along the ledge and was relieved to see the arachnid falling into the void below.

'Very good, but it won't be the last,' said the sorceress. 'I'll let his friends finish you off, Arthur Pendragon. It's not your destiny to die at my hand.'

She turned away. Arthur watched with horror as the torchlight faded into the distance. In the darkness he could hear the scurrying of many legs – more spiders were on their way. He had expected to face perils on his journey, but he'd never dreamed that there would be someone actually trying to stop him succeeding. How did this witch even know to find him here? Why was she doing this to him? Could it possibly be that she had engineered the whole thing – had she been responsible for the poison too?

'Who are you?' he yelled again – but there was no reply.

CHAPTER FIFTEEN
A GUIDING LIGHT

Gaius sat helplessly at Merlin's bedside. The boy was getting weaker by the moment, but the doctor could do nothing about it and it tore him up inside. Even Merlin's muttering of spells had ceased.

And then suddenly he spoke again, faintly but urgently, as if roused by a great need. 'Arthur . . . it's too dark . . .' He began to chant a spell, and Gaius was startled to see a ball of blue-white light appear in the unconscious boy's hand. At least

Gwen wasn't around to witness this – he would never be able to explain it.

'Arthur...follow the light...save yourself...' Merlin moaned.

Gaius stared at him, horrified. What strange nightmares was the boy's fevered brain dreaming up? he wondered.

For Arthur, of course, the nightmare was all too real. He hung there in the darkness, his

fingers clinging to the ledge, desperate to keep a hold. It was a few moments before he realized that the darkness was not quite so dark any more. There, above him, floated a blue-white ball of light. What new sorcery was this? Had the witch decided to finish him off after all?

The prince instinctively tried to duck out of its way, almost losing his grip as he did so. 'Come on then – what are you waiting for?' he yelled at the orb, expecting its evil magic to dispatch him at any moment. But instead, the light just floated higher, illuminating the ledge. Now that Arthur could see it properly, he was able to move his grip to a more stable spot – and, with an immense effort, he managed to swing his legs up onto solid ground again. The ball of light bobbed up higher, showing him handholds on the rock and, far above him, what might be a way out.

Arthur ignored the tempting path to safety. He could see that high up, just out of reach, was the Mortaeus plant — and the leaf that would cure Merlin.

But below him, the scurrying sound was getting louder. A thousand deadly spiders were swarming towards the prince.

The blue-white ball bobbed urgently, imploring Arthur to follow it. He knew he had to make a move now. Sending up a prayer, he leaped for a distant handhold — and made it. One arm reached up as high as it could go, his desperate fingers scrabbling for the Mortaeus flower and its single leaf. He stretched and stretched, trying to reach the plant without falling. At last he made it. With the precious leaf finally in his grasp, he breathed a sigh of relief — but his ordeal wasn't over yet. As he swung back towards the orb, he saw the spiders gaining on him from below. He had no choice but to trust the strange light. As it guided his way, he began to climb as fast as he could away from the deadly creatures.

At last he reached a fissure in the rock and felt the cool night breeze on his face. He scrambled through the opening, his hands now bleeding and raw, but he felt no triumph at his escape. He had survived – but Merlin's life would not be saved until the leaf was in Gaius' capable hands.

As the moon shone down on the exhausted prince, the ball of light turned to mist and faded away.

Back in Camelot, the ball of light disappeared from Merlin's hand. The young warlock stopped crying out to Arthur, stopped muttering the spells that had worried Gaius so much. But this was worse. All colour had left his cheeks. As Gaius bent over his charge, he could barely tell whether Merlin was even breathing.

'It's Arthur! Inform the king! Arthur's returned to Camelot!'

The cry went out as the prince rode towards the city. He was tired and hurt, but still sitting upright in the saddle. All that mattered was getting the leaf to Gaius.

As he crossed the drawbridge, guards stepped out in front of him, their pikes blocking his path. 'I'm sorry, sire,' said the captain. 'You are under arrest. By order of the king.'

Arthur had visited the dungeons many times, but being locked in a cell was a new experience for him. It was not a pleasant one. Even worse, his father had just arrived to visit. He hadn't hoped for praise from the king, he hadn't expected an apology, but Uther's anger went even further than he'd imagined.

'You disobeyed me!' Uther was yelling at his son.

'Of course I did.' Arthur would not let himself be cowed when he knew he had done the right thing. 'A man's life was at stake. Do not let Merlin die because of something I did.'

'Why do you care so much?' Uther asked. 'This boy is just a servant, not a nobleman.'

The prince had no idea how to get his father to understand. 'He knew the danger he was putting himself in; he knew what would happen if he drank from that goblet but he did it anyway. He saved my life.' Arthur changed tack, realizing that there was something very important the king had to know. 'There's more. There was a woman at the mountain – she knew I was there for the flower. I don't think it was

Bayard who tried to poison me.'

'Of course it was.' A haunted look had appeared in Uther's eyes, but his voice was dismissive.

Arthur gave up. There was no point in trying to get his father to listen right now. For the moment, all that really mattered was getting the anti-dote to Merlin. He reached inside his tunic and drew out the tiny flower and

leaf that had cost him so much effort and pain. 'Gaius knows what to do with it,' he said. 'Put me in the stocks for a week, a month even – I don't care. Just make sure it gets to him.' He held out his hand to his father. 'I'm begging you.'

Uther took the plant and the prince gave a sigh of relief. First Merlin must be saved. There would still be time to convince his father of Bayard's innocence and avert a war, even if he had to do it while rotten fruit was being thrown at him in the stocks.

But to Arthur's horror, the king held up his hand – and crushed the fragile plant.

'Don't!' the prince cried in anguish.

The king's face was hard. 'You have to learn – there is a right and a wrong way of doing things.' He stepped away from the cell door and let the crumpled bloom fall to the floor. 'I'll see you're let out in a week. Then you can find yourself another servant.'

As Uther strode from the dungeons, the prince of Camelot flung himself on his hands and knees, desperately reaching through the bars to scrabble for the tiny broken leaf.

CHAPTER SIXTEEN
GWEN TO THE RESCUE

Gaius was still sitting by Merlin's bedside. The boy's face was grey, and Gaius struggled to detect the shallow rise and fall of his chest that showed he was still alive. But the prince had returned – perhaps all might yet be well.

He looked up as Gwen entered, anxious for news. 'Does Arthur have the flower?'

Her eyes filled with tears as she took in Merlin's condition. 'I don't know. Uther won't allow anyone to see him.'

Gaius turned his face away, fearing he might weep too. 'Merlin doesn't have long. Only the leaf of the Mortaeus flower can save him.'

'Then we have to find out if Arthur has it. I could sneak into the dungeons.'

'That would be very dangerous.' And Gaius was well aware that the dungeons held very unhappy memories for Gwen too.

But danger hadn't stopped Arthur riding out to find the cure, and Gaius could see that even the thought of being thrown back in the dungeons wasn't going to stop Gwen from doing all she could to help. 'I've got to go,' she said simply. 'Merlin will die if I don't.'

Having been a prisoner herself, Gwen knew how things worked down in the cells. Bread and water were brought for the captives twice a day, and no one would think it odd if the Lady Morgana's maid waited on the prince – if the guards even recognized her.

She sneaked into the kitchens for suitable fare, and then hurried down to the dungeons. 'Food for the prisoner,' she told the guard, trying not to show her impatience as he fumbled for his keys to let her through the gate.

To her dismay, the guard followed her to Arthur's cell. Unable to talk to the prince, she just had to hope that he would realize why she was there. He looked up as she entered and she gazed back at him, her eyes pleading with him to understand.

He turned away, his manner cold. 'Set it down over there.'

She did so, her hopes dying. But then he gave a tiny nod, just for her, and her heart

leaped. Trying to act normally, she began
to walk out of the cell.

Arthur crossed over to the plate of food.
'Wait a minute!' he called after her, every
inch the imperious prince. 'I couldn't
possibly eat this, it's disgusting.' He put the
plate down on the floor, and Gwen hurried
over to pick it up. She was overjoyed to
see that now, by the bread, there was a
fragment of some strange plant.

She curtsied and left the cell. She
desperately wanted to run but couldn't
afford to create suspicion – not now she

was so close to success.

'You – wait!'

Gwen froze in horror as the guard called her back. She closed her eyes as he strode towards her. Then, even worse, he reached for the plate . . .

. . . and took a piece of bread. 'Waste not, want not, eh?' he said with a grin.

She smiled back and started on her way again. Through the gate, up the corridor. At the bottom of the stairs . . .

. . . a serving girl passed the other way, carrying bread and water. Gwen quickened her pace, realizing what was coming.

'Food for Prince Arthur,' she heard the girl say.

'You! Stay where you are!' came the guard's shout.

Gwen grabbed the Mortaeus plant, dropped the plate, and ran as she had never run before.

CHAPTER SEVENTEEN
GAIUS THE SORCERER

Gaius sprang up as Gwen entered and snatched the plant from her. As she sank down on a chair, exhausted, he removed the leaf and placed it in a pestle and mortar with some other herbs that he'd already prepared.

He lifted the pestle to grind the ingredients together – and his hand froze in midair. A terrible thought had struck him.

'Why've you stopped?' Gwen cried.

'The poison was created using magic,' he told her. 'We may need magic to make an antidote.'

'But we can't!' Her eyes were wide with disbelief. 'It's forbidden, even if we could . . .'

Gaius nodded. He knew what he had to do – but Gwen must not be involved. He shouldn't have said anything; shouldn't give her the faintest reason to suspect the huge risk he was about to take – but in the shock of realization he had spoken without thinking. Now he had to get the girl out of the way – and quickly. 'I'll try to make it work without,' he said. 'But I need some fresh water. Gwen, please . . . ?'

Tired as she was, she jumped up instantly and hurried away, giving a last, fearful look at the silent boy on the bed.

Gaius raised the mortar, grasping it firmly

in both hands, and attempted to whisper an incantation – but he found that his voice wouldn't work.

Gaius had served the king loyally and faithfully for over twenty years – and then Merlin had come along. Suddenly the doctor had found himself harbouring a warlock. Still, Gaius knew he was acting for the best, although Uther himself would not see it like that.

But actually to cast magic *himself* – to disobey the king's most fundamental law . . .

It was an enormous step to take, and Gaius was scared.

He was serving the king and the kingdom, but he had to utterly betray Uther to do so. For such a loyal subject, this was the most difficult thing of all.

There was another worry too. 'Magic corrupts,' he'd told Merlin, not that long ago. Once he'd stepped over that line again, would he ever be able to go back?

But of course, he knew he had to do it. Whatever the consequences. Even if he hadn't already come to love Merlin as a son, even if Merlin wasn't destined to be a great warlock, Gaius had promised the boy's mother he would look after him. The doctor drew in a breath, and began the spell again. As the enchantment flowed over it, the green paste of leaf and herbs bubbled and fizzed and then turned crystal clear.

Gwen ran in with a pitcher of water. Gaius took it from her with a word of thanks and poured some into the mortar, mixing it with the paste to make a thin liquid. Then he knelt down beside Merlin.

'Hold his nose – he has to swallow this,' he told Gwen as he gently opened the boy's mouth and poured in the antidote.

They waited anxiously. How quickly would it work?

Gwen gave a cry of horror. 'He's stopped breathing! What's happening? Gaius, what's happening?'

The doctor put his ear to Merlin's chest, listening for a heartbeat, trying to detect the faintest sound or hint of movement. There was nothing, and Gaius suddenly felt like an old, old man. 'His heart has stopped.'

'He's dead?' Gwen's voice was dull with shock.

But Gaius refused to believe the evidence of his

senses. 'He can't be!' he cried. 'It was his destiny . . .' Merlin was supposed to achieve so much, have a great future ahead of him – this just couldn't have happened!

'It's my fault,' sobbed Gwen. 'If I'd got here sooner, if I'd been quicker . . .'

Gaius shook his head. 'No, it was me. I should've looked after him better – it's my fault . . .'

Gwen held out her arms and the physician hugged her, both united in their grief. How could this be true? How could Merlin be dead?

'That's disgusting,' said a voice. 'You're old enough to be her grandfather.'

'Merlin!' They spun round in amazement, their faces lit up with joy.
'Merlin, you're alive!'

'No, I'm a ghost come back to haunt you,' he began, but

suddenly found he couldn't speak – Gwen was grabbing him, pulling him to her, kissing him on the lips. Even after she'd stopped, looking a bit stunned at what she'd just done, Merlin found it hard to form any words.

'Sorry,' Gwen said anxiously. 'I'm just . . . I thought you were dead.'

'It's fine,' Merlin managed at last. 'It's more than fine . . .'

Gaius cleared his throat. Merlin tore his eyes from Gwen and turned to him. 'Er, what happened?' he asked the doctor. 'The last thing I remember is drinking the wine . . .'

Gaius looked at Gwen and raised his eyebrows. This was going to be a *long* story.

CHAPTER EIGHTEEN
WAR AVERTED

Uther was holding a council of war. Word of Bayard's arrest had got back to Mercia, and forces were closing in on Camelot. The king was in no mood for interruptions, and waved Gaius away angrily as the elderly doctor entered the room. However, Gaius ignored him. 'Sire, forgive me,' he said, 'but may I speak with you?'

The king shook his head. 'Not now.'

'Please, your highness, it's important. And

what I have to tell you may have some bearing on your plans. I know who tried to poison Arthur.'

Uther rose from the table and took Gaius to one side. 'So do I,' he hissed. 'He's locked in my dungeons.'

'It wasn't Bayard,' Gaius told him. 'The poison was magical and I'd recognize the hand that made it anywhere . . . Nimueh.'

'You must be mistaken.' The king didn't want to hear this. 'Have you any proof?'

'The poison used against Merlin was made more potent by the use of magic.'

The king took Gaius' arm again and

led him even further away from the other councillors, although they were speaking so softly that no one could have overheard. 'You're saying that Nimueh conspired with Bayard to kill Arthur?'

'No. Bayard's innocent.' Gaius gestured over at the central table, where the plans for war were being made. 'This is what she wanted all along – a war to bring strife and misery to Camelot.'

Uther raised his voice and called over to the councillors. 'How long before Bayard's armies reach our walls?'

'A day, maybe less,' answered his captain.

'We should send our cavalry out to meet them.'

The king paused, considering. Gaius held his breath, waiting for his decision.

'Instruct your men not to leave Camelot until I give the word.'

The doctor gave a sigh of relief. Then he summoned his courage to ask Uther a question. 'Do you think Arthur should be told the truth about Nimueh?'

Uther's face was hard. The king and the physician shared a secret about Nimueh, a secret they had guarded for many years. Uther's reaction made Gaius suspect that no other person would learn it for many years to come – if ever.

Some time later, the king stood on the castle battlements, watching his freed prisoners ride away from Camelot. There would be no war. Bayard had accepted Uther's apologies, and the peace treaty would go ahead.

Arthur and Morgana stood a little to one side. This was the first chance they'd had to speak since the prince had been released from the cells. 'OK, let the bragging begin – how did you manage it?' Morgana asked with a smile.

But Arthur wasn't going to brag. 'I'm not sure,' he said honestly. 'All I know is that I had help. Someone knew I was in trouble and sent a light to guide the way.'

'Who?' asked Morgana, casting an anxious glance over her shoulder – but the king hadn't heard.

'I don't know,' Arthur replied. 'Whoever it was, I'm only here because of them.'

She smiled at him. 'I'm glad you're back,' she told him. Then she turned and went inside.

Arthur was alone with his father. But to the prince's surprise, when Uther spoke to him there was little trace of the cold, cruel man

who had thrown him into the dungeons.
If it were possible – but of course it wasn't
– Arthur might almost have thought the
king sounded nervous as he asked, 'That
woman you met in the forest – what did
she tell you?'

Arthur shrugged. 'Not much – she was
too busy trying to get me killed. It was
strange, though. I was at her mercy. She
could've finished me off but she chose not
to. She said it wasn't my destiny to die at
her hand.'

'You must've been scared,' Uther said
gently.

Arthur wasn't used to compassion from
his father. 'It had its moments,' he said.

'Those who practise magic know only
evil; they despise and seek to destroy
goodness wherever they find it,' said the
king. 'Which is why she wanted you dead.
She is evil.'

'It sounds as if you know her,' Arthur said with some surprise.

'I do.'

The prince couldn't quite believe his ears. How could it possibly be that his father knew this witch, this embodiment of everything he hated most?

But the answer, when it came, was a disappointment. 'To know the heart of one sorcerer is to know them all,' Uther said. He put a hand on Arthur's shoulder. 'You did the right thing, even though you were disobeying me. I'm proud of you, Arthur – never forget that.'

And Arthur was so surprised, so pleased, to receive praise from the king that he didn't for a second consider that Uther might not have been telling him the whole truth about Nimueh . . .

By that evening Merlin, although still weak,

was able to get out of bed. Gaius was busy preparing a meal – he insisted that the boy needed to eat to get his strength back.

Gaius had told him about Kara's true identity and Arthur's mission to find the antidote, although he didn't know all the details. For a moment Merlin had a strange flash of memory – a vision of Arthur in a cave – but dismissed it as a fever dream, and forgot it again almost straight away.

He felt incredibly grateful to Arthur, but a little embarrassed too. There were moments when they seemed to be close, he and the prince, and he knew there was no malice in Arthur's teasing – but surely a prince and a servant could never be real friends? The thing was, almost without realizing it, Merlin had come to admire Arthur – he no longer had any trouble believing the Great Dragon's prediction that Arthur would become a remarkable king. Merlin was prepared to die to make that happen. What he hadn't bargained for was that Arthur would be willing to risk his life in return. He could sense that this was something big; that the bond tying him to Arthur connected them more closely than he'd imagined.

But he also knew that they would never be able to put any of this into words, or even acknowledge it to each other.

So when Arthur put his head round the door to say, 'Still alive then?' Merlin only said, 'Just about – I understand I have you to thank for that.'

The prince shrugged. 'Yeah, well, it was nothing. A half-decent servant is hard to come by. I was only dropping by to make sure you were all right, check you'd be back to work tomorrow . . .'

'Yeah, of course. Bright and early.' And then, because he felt he had to at

least make the effort and acknowledge what had happened, Merlin said, 'Arthur . . . thank you.'

Arthur smiled, slightly uncomfortable as well. 'You too. Get some rest.' And he walked out, leaving Merlin to his supper.

Gaius came over and placed a bowl of soup on the table. Merlin suddenly thought of something else. 'You know, all that Arthur did – it would've been for nothing if you hadn't known how to make the antidote.'

Now it was the doctor's turn to look embarrassed. He wasn't going to tell the boy just what making the antidote had cost him. 'Eat your dinner,' he said.

'I still don't understand,' Merlin said after a while, 'why Nimueh went to all the trouble of framing Bayard. She could've just kept quiet and killed Arthur with the poison.'

He wasn't prepared at all for Gaius' answer. 'Destroying Arthur and Camelot wasn't all she was after. Remember whom she got to accuse Bayard of poisoning? She knew you'd be forced to drink the wine. It was *you* she wanted to kill.'

Merlin stared, his spoon frozen halfway to his mouth.

'It seems that someone else knows you're destined for great things. I don't think we've seen the last of Nimueh.'

Merlin couldn't quite believe it. When he'd

left his village to come here to Camelot, he'd never dreamed that life would become so dangerous.

But then again, he hadn't dreamed he'd find so many good friends here, either.

If Nimueh tried anything again – they'd be ready for her.

THE MAGIC BEGINS

Merlin arrives in Camelot full of excitement
and eager for adventure. But sorcery is
outlawed here and so he must learn
to hide his own magical talents.

When a mysterious new knight turns up
for the sword tournament, Merlin suspects
that dark magic is involved. He's determined
to investigate, but soon finds that keeping the
magic secret – and Prince Arthur alive –
is much harder than he thought . . .

978 0 553 82111 6

COMING SOON

A FIGHTING CHANCE

Merlin wants to help his new friend,
Lancelot, become a Knight of Camelot
– but it's not as easy as he hopes.

Then the Lady Morgana is struck down
by a mystery illness. Gaius is baffled and a
new physician arrives to help. He seems to
have all the answers, but Merlin suspects that
there's something sinister going on.

978 0 553 82501 5

SWORD AND SORCERY

When Merlin and Morgana join forces to save a child the king has commanded be put to death, they soon discover that going against King Uther could prove fatal.

Meanwhile, a mysterious black knight arrives to challenge the Knights of Camelot to mortal combat. Old secrets, long hidden, are stirring and the king is afraid for his only son. The black knight seems invincible and Merlin senses that only magic can stop him . . .

978 0 553 82502 2

ALSO AVAILABLE

MERLIN: THE COMPLETE GUIDE

Explore Merlin's world and find out all there
is to know about the characters and their
secrets. With facts and great imagery of all
the cast, locations and props. Discover the
lore and legend of Merlin!

Never seen before footage as well as maps
and spells from the spell book finish this
complete guide. It's a must have for any
Merlin fan!

978 0 553 82108 6

ALSO AVAILABLE

MERLIN MYSTERY ACTIVITY BOOK

A mysterious stranger has taken Arthur prisoner and Merlin has to find him and set him free. Join Merlin on a dangerous journey to save Arthur. Work through the puzzles, play the games and answer the riddles to help Merlin save his friend, the future king of Camelot.

This activity book includes a free spell notebook!

978 0 553 82105 5

ALSO AVAILABLE

MERLIN QUEST ACTIVITY BOOK

This Quest Activity book sets the stage for tournament day in Camelot. But danger lurks around every corner. An evil knight threatens Arthur, can he defeat him in battle? Join Arthur and his friends on their adventure around Camelot. Solve the puzzles, play the games and answer the riddles to help Arthur defeat the evil knight and win the tournament.

This activity book includes a free pull-out game!

978 0 553 82106 2

THE DRAGON'S CALL

When Merlin arrives in the great kingdom
of Camelot he discovers a dark side to the
bustling city: magic is outlawed on pain of
death! If he wants to stay alive, Merlin will
have to keep his unique magical talents a
closely guarded secret . . .

978 0 553 82109 3

VALIANT

A mysterious new knight arrives in Camelot
for the sword tournament. His fighting skills
are impressive but when an opponent is not
just injured but *poisoned*, Merlin suspects that
dark magic is involved. Merlin is determined
to expose the evil, but Arthur is next in line
to fight and time is running out . . .

978 0 553 82110 9

THE MARK OF NIMUEH

A deadly plague rages through
Camelot and it seems that sorcery is the
only explanation. When Gwen is arrested
for witchcraft, Merlin knows the wrong
person is accused, but can he uncover
the truth, find a cure and save his
friend from execution?

978 0 553 82114 7

COMING SOON
FOR OLDER READERS

THE POISONED
CHALICE

The sorceress Nimueh is weaving a
spell with powerful dark magic.
Her target is Merlin . . .

978 0 553 82115 4